20¢

WALT DISNEY'S

Snow White

AND THE SEVEN DWARFS

ADAPTED FROM

GRIMM'S FAIRY TALES

ILLUSTRATIONS BY

THE WALT DISNEY STUDIO

Adapted by Ken O'Brien and Al Dempster from the Walt Disney Motion Picture "Snow White and the Seven Dwarfs"

GOLDEN PRESS
Western Publishing Company, Inc.
Racine, Wisconsin

This Little Golden Book was produced under the supervision of

THE WALT DISNEY STUDIO

The Little Golden Books here bring you, in gay color, delightful stories and illustrations adapted from the world-famous Walt Disney Motion Pictures. In them you will find Pinocchio, The Three Little Pigs, Bambi, Dumbo, Uncle Remus, Cinderella, Alice in Wonderland, Peter Pan, and many other well-loved Disney characters.

Forty-Second Printing, 1977

Produced in U.S.A. by Western Publishing Company, Inc.

ONCE UPON A TIME, long, long ago, a lovely Queen sat by her window sewing. As she worked she thought, "If only I had a little daughter, how happy I would be."

Dreaming, she pricked her finger with her needle. Three drops of blood fell on the snow-white linen.

"How lovely my little girl would be if she had lips as red as blood, skin as white as snow and hair as black as ebony," thought the Queen.

Some time later, a little daughter was born to the Queen, and she was just as beautiful as the Queen had hoped she might be.

The happy mother decided to call her baby Snow White.

But the Queen was very ill, and when Snow White was still a little girl, her mother died.

Snow White's father, the King, was broken hearted. For many years he was sad and lonely.

But at last the lonely King married again, and there was great rejoicing in the land.

His new Queen was very beautiful to look upon, but alas, her heart was cold and cruel.

The Queen was vain, too. She would spend hours dressing herself in fine clothes, and brushing her black hair. Then she would stand by the mirror and admire herself.

She was so vain that she wanted to be the most beautiful woman in the kingdom.

Now the Queen's most prized possession was a magic mirror. Every day she asked it:

Mirror, mirror on the wall,
Who is the fairest of us all?

If the mirror replied that she was the fairest in the land, the Queen was happy, and all was well.

But sometimes another lady was named. Then the Queen would fly into such a terrible rage that the people around her trembled with fear. And the wicked Queen would order the poor lady to be killed.

Meanwhile, Snow White was growing up to be more and more beautiful. And as well as being pretty, she was so sweet natured that everyone loved her—everyone but the Queen.

The Queen looked at Snow White jealously. At last she could stand the sight of the lovely Princess no longer. She banished Snow White to the servants' quarters.

Snow White's fine clothes were taken away from her, and she had to dress in rags like the other servants.

And like the other servants, Snow White had to work very hard. She slaved from early morning until late at night, scrubbing and cleaning the palace floors, washing the dishes, sewing and mending the Queen's clothes.

As she worked, she would sing so sweetly that the birds would come to listen to her voice.

"She will soon lose her beauty," thought the wicked Queen. "For who can call her lovely in her old rags, and with her hands roughened by work?"

Nevertheless, the Queen went to her mirror and day after day asked the same question:

Mirror, mirror on the wall,
Who is the fairest of us all?

The wicked, vain Queen was still afraid that one day Snow White would grow up to be more beautiful than anyone else in the land.

While she worked, Snow White dreamed beautiful daydreams about a handsome Prince. Some day, she knew, he would come and carry her off to his castle in the clouds.

It seemed to the jealous Queen, as she watched Snow White, that the Princess grew in loveliness as each day passed.

And indeed, though Snow White wore ragged clothes, her beauty was plain to see.

At last came the day the Queen had been dreading.

Mirror, mirror on the wall,
Who is the fairest of us all?

she said. And the mirror replied:

Her lips blood red, her hair like night,
Her skin like snow, her name—Snow White!

The angry Queen called her huntsman to her.

"Take the Princess into the forest and bring me back her heart in this jeweled box," she said.

The huntsman bowed his head in grief. He had no choice but to obey the Queen's command.

OFF INTO THE FOREST went Snow White and the huntsman next day. The Princess, not knowing what was in store for her, skipped along beside the huntsman, now stopping to pick violets, now singing a happy tune.

At last the huntsman, heartbroken, fell to his knees beside the Princess.

"I cannot kill you, Princess," he said, "even though it is the Queen's command. Run into the forest and hide, and never return to the castle."

Alone in the forest, Snow White wept with fright. But she was not really alone, she found. All the little woodland animals were her friends. And, chirping and chattering happily, they led her to a new home.

It was a sweet little, tiny little house in the woods the animals showed Snow White. But no one was home, and when she looked in the window, my, what an untidy sight met her eyes! The sink was piled with unwashed dishes, and everything was thickly blanketed with dust.

"Maybe the children who live here need someone to keep house for them," said Snow White. "Let's clean their house."

So in they went. And with the help of her new forest friends, Snow White soon had that little house spic and span.

Then she went upstairs and fell asleep across the seven little beds.

As she slept, home from work came the seven little men who lived in that house in the woods.

Hi-ho, hi-ho,
It's home from work we go!

sang the seven little men—the Seven Dwarfs.

Then they saw their little house, just as Snow White had seen it. But they knew at once that something was changed! It was clean!

Up the stairs crept the Seven Dwarfs. And there they found Snow White just waking up.

"Oh!" cried Snow White. "I know who you are." She had read their names on their beds. "You're Dopey and Sneezy and Happy and Grumpy and Doc and Bashful and Sleepy!"

Snow White told the Dwarfs about the wicked Queen's plot, and they insisted that she must stay with them.

"Supper is not quite ready yet," said Snow White, who was very pleased to be asked to stay. "You'll just have time to wash."

"Wash?" cried all the little men. They had almost forgotten what the word meant. But they were soon scrubbed clean, and even Grumpy got a soaking.

The Seven Dwarfs soon grew to love Snow White and her merry ways.

The next morning, instead of going to work in their mine, the Seven Dwarfs decided to make a beautiful new bed for Snow White.

The seven little men would not have worked so happily if they could have seen beyond the forest. The wicked Queen had learned that Snow White was still alive. And now, disguised as an old woman, she was making her way to their very own house, with a poisoned apple for Snow White!

When the Dwarfs had left Snow White that morning they had warned her to stay in the house.

"Be careful of strangers!" Grumpy had said, as Snow White kissed him good-by.

And Snow White had promised that she would be careful.

Later that day the old woman knocked at her door.

Alas! Snow White could not resist the magic

apple. She took one bite, and sank lifeless to the floor.

Hurrying away, the wicked Queen fell into a deep chasm, and was never seen again. But that did not bring Snow White back to life.

The sorrowing Dwarfs laid her upon a bed of gold and crystal, and kept watch over her night and day.

One day a handsome Prince came to the forest and saw Snow White. Charmed with her beauty, he kissed her. At last Snow White awoke! The Seven Dwarfs danced with joy, and the Prince carried her off to his castle in the clouds.